Christian Meditation Guide

Tracy McNeil

Contents

Introduction

Finding moments of true stillness and connection with God can seem like an impossible task, especially in our fast-paced, noise-filled world. Our minds race from one thought to the next, our phones buzz with constant notifications, and our to-do lists seem never-ending. Yet, amidst this chaos, there exists a powerful, time-honoured practice that can transform our spiritual lives and deepen our relationship with God: meditation.

But what exactly is Christian meditation? For many, the word "meditation" might conjure images of cross-legged yogis chanting or New Age practitioners seeking to empty their minds. However, Christian meditation is something entirely different and profoundly life-changing. It's not about emptying our minds, but rather filling them with the truth and wisdom of God's Word. It's not about achieving a state of nothingness, but about entering into a rich, vibrant conversation with our Creator.

At the heart of Christian meditation lies the Word of God, which Hebrews 4:12 describes as *"living and active, sharper than any two-edged sword, piercing to the division of soul and of spirit, of joints and of marrow, and discerning the thoughts and intentions of the heart"* (ESV). This verse reveals the dynamic power of Scripture - it's not just ancient text, but a living force that can penetrate the deepest parts of our being. When we meditate on God's Word, we're not merely engaging in a mental exercise, but opening ourselves to a transformative encounter with the Divine.

Furthermore, 2 Timothy 3:16 reminds us that *"All Scripture is breathed out by God and profitable for teaching, for reproof, for correction, and for training in righteousness"* (ESV). This verse underscores the purpose and value of meditating on Scripture. As we contemplate God's Word, we're not just gaining information, but receiving divine instruction, correction, and guidance for righteous living.

The practice of meditation has deep roots in the Judaeo-Christian tradition. From the ancient Israelites to Jesus himself, meditation on God's Word has been a cornerstone of faithful living. The Psalmist declares, *"I will meditate on your precepts and fix my eyes on your ways"* (Psalm 119:15, ESV). Joshua was instructed to meditate on the Book of the Law day and night to ensure his success and prosperity (Joshua 1:8). These are not casual suggestions, but divine imperatives that speak to the transformative power of biblical meditation.

In this book, we will embark on a journey to rediscover this ancient practice and learn how to apply it in our modern lives. We'll explore the rich meaning of meditation as understood in the Hebrew language and throughout Scripture. We'll uncover the profound benefits that come from regularly meditating on God's Word – benefits that touch not just our spiritual lives, but our emotional and mental well-being as well.

More than just theory, this book offers practical guidance. You'll find a step-by-step approach to developing a meaningful meditation practice, with tips and techniques to help you overcome common obstacles and make meditation a natural part of your daily walk with God.

We'll also address an important topic that often causes confusion: the difference between Christian meditation and New Age practices. Understanding these distinctions is crucial for maintaining the purity and power of biblical meditation in a world that often co-opts spiritual practices for non-Christian purposes.

Whether you're new to the concept of Christian meditation or looking to deepen your existing practice, this book is designed to meet you where you are. It's my hope that by the final page, you'll not only understand the what and why of biblical meditation, but you'll be equipped with the how - ready to embark on a transformative journey of contemplating, internalizing, and living out God's Word.

So, let's quiet our hearts, open our minds, and prepare to dive deep into the life-changing practice of Christian meditation. As we learn to be still and know that He is God (Psalm 46:10), we'll discover a wellspring of spiritual growth, peace, and intimacy with our Creator that we may never have thought possible.

Are you ready to begin? Let's turn the page and start this exciting journey together, guided by the living and active Word of God, which is profitable for every aspect of our spiritual growth.

1

Meaning of Meditation

Meditation, in its Christian context, is a profound and transformative spiritual practice that has its roots in ancient biblical tradition. To fully understand the depth and significance of meditation in Christianity, we must explore its meaning in the Hebrew context, its general understanding within the faith, and the scriptural foundations that support and encourage this practice.

Hebrew Context

In the Hebrew Bible or Old Testament, several words are used to describe the concept of meditation. Two of the most significant are "hagah" and "siyach".

1. Hagah: This word appears 25 times in the Hebrew Bible and is often translated as "meditate," "mutter," or "ponder." Its root meaning suggests a low sound, like the growling of a lion over its prey or the cooing of a dove. In the context of spiritual practice, hagah implies a deep, internal process of repeating and pondering God's word.

For example, in Joshua 1:8, we read: "*This Book of the Law shall not depart from your mouth, but you shall meditate (hagah) on it day and night, so that you may be careful to do according to all that is written in it.*" Here, meditation is presented as a continuous, active engagement with God's law.

2. Siyach: This word appears 20 times in the Hebrew Bible and can be translated as "meditate," "complain," or "talk." It carries the idea of thoughtful contemplation or pouring out one's heart.

Psalm 119:15 uses this word: "*I will meditate (siyach) on your precepts and fix my eyes on your ways.*" This verse portrays meditation as a focused contemplation on God's teachings.

The use of these words in Hebrew scriptures reveals that biblical meditation is not about emptying the mind, but rather filling it with God's word and deeply pondering its meaning and application.

In the broader Christian context, meditation is understood as a deliberate, focused reflection on God's word, His character, and His works. Unlike some Eastern forms of meditation that aim to empty the mind, Christian meditation seeks to fill the mind with divine truth and align one's thoughts with God's will.

Christian meditation involves:

3. Active engagement: It's not a passive state but an active process of thinking, reflecting, and internalizing spiritual truths.

4. God-centered focus: The object of meditation is always God, His word, or His works, not self or abstract concepts.

5. Transformative purpose: The goal is spiritual growth, deeper understanding, and closer communion with God.

6. Integration with prayer: Meditation often intertwines with prayer, as one reflects on God's word and responds in conversation with Him.

7. Practical application: True biblical meditation leads to changed behavior and attitudes, not just intellectual understanding.

Scriptures About Meditation

The Bible contains numerous references to meditation, highlighting its importance in the spiritual life of believers. Let's examine some key passages:

1. Joshua 1:8 - "This Book of the Law shall not depart from your mouth, but you shall meditate on it day and night, so that you may be careful to do according to all that is written in it. For then you will make your way prosperous, and then you will have good success."

This verse emphasizes the continuous nature of meditation and its practical outcome in obedience and success.

2. Psalm 1:1-2 - "Blessed is the man who walks not in the counsel of the wicked, nor stands in the way of sinners, nor sits in the seat of scoffers; but his delight is in the law of the Lord, and on his law he meditates day and night."

Here, meditation is presented as a characteristic of the righteous person, contrasted with those who follow worldly ways.

3. Psalm 19:14 - "Let the words of my mouth and the meditation of my heart be acceptable in your sight, O Lord, my rock and my redeemer."

This prayer reflects the psalmist's desire for his inner reflections to be pleasing to God, showing that meditation is a matter of the heart.

4. Psalm 119:97 - "Oh how I love your law! It is my meditation all the day."

Throughout Psalm 119, the longest chapter in the Bible, the psalmist repeatedly expresses his love for God's law and his commitment to meditating on it.

5. Philippians 4:8 - "Finally, brothers, whatever is true, whatever is honorable, whatever is just, whatever is pure, whatever is lovely, whatever is commendable, if there is any excellence, if there is anything worthy of praise, think about these things."

While not using the word "meditate," this New Testament verse encourages focused reflection on virtuous and godly things, embodying the essence of Christian meditation.

These scriptures reveal that meditation is not an optional extra in the Christian life, but a fundamental practice for spiritual growth and maturity.

2

Meditating on God's Word

Meditating on God's Word is a transformative spiritual practice that has been embraced by believers for centuries. It goes beyond mere reading or studying the Bible; it's an intentional, focused reflection on Scripture that allows God's truth to penetrate our hearts and minds deeply. Let's explore the profound meaning of biblical meditation, its numerous benefits for our spiritual lives, and a comprehensive guide on how to incorporate this practice into your daily walk with God. Whether you're new to the concept of meditating on Scripture or looking to deepen your existing practice, this chapter will equip you with the knowledge and tools to engage more fully with God's Word and experience its life-changing power.

The Meaning of Meditating on God's Word

To truly understand what it means to meditate on God's Word, we must first distinguish it from other forms of Bible engagement and secular meditation practices.

Meditation in the biblical sense is not about emptying our minds or achieving a state of detached awareness. Instead, it's about filling our minds with God's truth and actively engaging with His Word. The Hebrew word most commonly used for meditation in the Old Testament is "hagah," which can be translated as to mutter, speak, or ponder. This gives us a picture of someone repeating God's words to themselves, turning them over in their minds, and deeply considering their meaning and application.

When we meditate on Scripture, we're not simply reading it passively or studying it academically. We're allowing it to sink into our hearts, examining it from various angles, and considering how it applies to our lives. It's a process of internalization, where God's Word becomes a part of us, shaping our thoughts, attitudes, and actions.

Meditating on God's Word involves focused attention on a verse, reciting the Scripture multiple times, and allowing its words to resonate within us, thinking deeply about the meaning of the text and its implications, and finally, engaging in a dialogue with God about His Word, asking for understanding and guidance.

This practice is fundamentally different from reading or studying the Bible, though these are also valuable activities. When we read the Bible, we often cover larger portions of text, gaining an overview of God's message. Studying involves analyzing the historical context, linguistic nuances, and theological implications of Scripture. While both reading and studying are crucial for biblical literacy, meditation takes us a step further by helping us internalize and personalize God's Word.

Meditating on God's Word is about creating space for the Holy Spirit to speak to us through Scripture, allowing it to challenge, comfort, and transform us. It's a way of abiding in Christ (John 15:7) and letting His words abide in us, shaping our very being.

The Benefits of Meditating on God's Word

The practice of meditating on Scripture offers numerous benefits for our spiritual, emotional, and even physical well-being. Let's explore some of the key advantages of incorporating this discipline into our lives:

a) **Deeper Understanding of God's Truth:** When we meditate on Scripture, we move beyond surface-level comprehension to a profound understanding of God's truth. By dwelling on His Word, we allow the Holy Spirit to illuminate its meaning, revealing layers of insight we might miss with casual reading. This deeper understanding helps us grasp God's character, His will, and His ways more fully.

b) **Spiritual Growth and Transformation:** Regular meditation on God's Word is a catalyst for spiritual growth. As we reflect on Scripture, it challenges our assumptions, convicts us of sin, and inspires us to greater faithfulness. Romans 12:2 encourages us to *"be transformed by the renewing of your mind,"* and meditating on God's Word is a powerful way to facilitate this renewal. It helps align our thoughts and attitudes with God's truth, leading to genuine transformation.

c) **Strengthened Faith and Trust in God:** As we meditate on God's promises, His faithfulness, and His character as revealed in Scripture, our faith is strengthened. We're reminded of God's power, love, and trustworthiness, which helps us face life's challenges with greater confidence in Him. Psalm 119:114 declares, *"You are my* *hiding place and my shield; I hope in your word."* Regular meditation reinforces this hope.

d) **Improved Ability to Resist Temptation:** Jesus Himself used Scripture to combat temptation in the wilderness (Matthew 4:1-11). When we meditate on God's Word, we're storing up truth in our hearts that can be recalled in moments of temptation. As Psalm 119:11 says, *"I have stored up your word in my heart, that I might not sin against you."* This internalized truth becomes a powerful defense against sin.

e) **Enhanced Prayer Life:** Meditating on Scripture enriches our prayer life by giving us God's own words to pray back to Him. It helps align our prayers with God's will and character, making our communication with Him more meaningful and effective. As we reflect on God's Word, we're often moved to respond in prayer, deepening our conversation with Him.

f) **Increased Peace and Reduced Anxiety:** In a world full of stress and uncertainty, meditating on God's Word can be a source of profound peace. Philippians 4:6-7 promises that as we bring our concerns to God, His peace will guard our hearts and minds. Dwelling on scriptures that remind us of God's love, care, and sovereignty can significantly reduce anxiety and promote emotional well-being.

g) **Improved Focus and Mental Clarity:** The practice of meditation helps train our minds to focus, which can benefit other areas of our lives. As we learn to concentrate on Scripture, we may find our ability to focus on other tasks improves as well. This mental discipline can lead to greater productivity and effectiveness in our daily lives.

h) **Deeper Intimacy with God:** Perhaps the most significant benefit of meditating on God's Word is the deeper intimacy it fosters with God Himself. As we spend time reflecting on His Word, we're essentially spending quality time with Him, listening to His heart and allowing Him to speak into our lives. This practice helps us know God more personally and experience His presence more fully.

i) **Guidance for Decision-Making:** As we internalize God's Word through meditation, we develop a biblical world view that informs our choices and actions. Psalm 119:105 describes God's Word as "a lamp to my feet and a light to my path." Regular meditation on Scripture equips us to make decisions that align with God's will and wisdom.

j) **Comfort in Times of Difficulty:** During challenging times, the truths we've meditated on can provide tremendous comfort and strength. Having God's promises and truths deeply rooted in our hearts through consistent meditation gives us a reservoir of hope and encouragement to draw from when we face trials.

By consistently engaging in the practice of meditating on God's Word, we open ourselves to these transformative benefits, allowing Scripture to shape our lives in profound and lasting ways.

A Step-by-Step Guide to Meditating on God's Word

Now that we understand the meaning and benefits of meditating on Scripture, let's explore a practical, step-by-step approach to incorporating this powerful practice into our daily lives.

Step 1: Prepare Your Heart and Mind

Before you begin meditating on God's Word, it's important to prepare yourself spiritually and mentally. Find a quiet place where you won't be disturbed. Take a few deep breaths and consciously set aside distractions. Pray, asking God to open your heart and mind to His Word. You might use a prayer like Psalm 119:18: *"Open my eyes, that I may behold wondrous things out of your law."*

Step 2: Choose a Scripture Passage

Select a portion of Scripture to meditate on. When you're starting out, it's often helpful to choose a shorter passage – perhaps a single verse or a small paragraph. As you grow more comfortable with the practice, you might choose to meditate on longer passages. Some good starting points include Psalms (e.g., Psalm 23, Psalm 1, Psalm 46), Proverbs, The Beatitudes (Matthew 5:3-12), Philippians 4:4-9, Colossians 3:12-17, and lots more.

Step 3: Read the Passage Slowly and Thoughtfully

Read your chosen passage slowly, preferably aloud. Pay attention to each word, letting them sink in. You might want to read it several times, perhaps emphasizing different words each time. This helps you notice nuances you might otherwise miss.

Step 4: Reflect on the Meaning

Now, start to think deeply about what you've read.

Ask yourself questions like:

What does this passage say about God's character?

What does it reveal about human nature?

Are there any promises, commands, or warnings in this passage?

What did this passage mean to its original audience?

How does this passage fit into the larger story of the Bible?

Don't rush this step. Allow yourself time to ponder these questions and see what insights emerge.

Step 5: Personalize the Scripture

Consider how this passage applies to your own life. Ask yourself:

How does this truth relate to my current circumstances?

Is there an attitude or action I need to change based on this Scripture?

How can I put this teaching into practice?

What comfort or encouragement does this passage offer me?

Step 6: Pray and Listen

Turn your reflections into a conversation with God. Pray about what you've read and the insights you've gained. Ask God to help you apply His Word to your life. Then, spend some time in silence, listening for God's voice. He may bring additional scriptures to mind, give you a sense of peace, or prompt you toward a specific action.

Step 7: Memorize Key Verses

If possible, try to memorize a key verse or phrase from your chosen passage. This allows you to carry God's Word with you throughout the day, continuing to meditate on it even when you don't have your Bible at hand.

Step 8: Journal Your Thoughts

Writing down your reflections can be a powerful way to process what God is teaching you through His Word. Note any insights, questions, or applications that came to mind during your meditation. This journal can become a valuable record of your spiritual journey.

Step 9: Live It Out

The ultimate goal of meditating on God's Word is not just to gain knowledge, but to be transformed. Look for opportunities throughout your day to put into practice what you've meditated on. This might involve changing an attitude, making a different choice, or taking a specific action.

Practical Tips for Establishing a Regular Meditation Practice

1. Set a specific time: Choose a consistent time each day for your meditation practice. Many find early morning works best, but choose a time that fits your schedule.

2. Start small: Begin with just 10-15 minutes of meditation and gradually increase the time as you become more comfortable with the practice.

3. Use aids: Some people find it helpful to use tools like devotional books, Scripture meditation apps, or guided audio meditations to support their practice.

4. Be patient: Like any skill, meditating on God's Word takes practice. Don't get discouraged if your mind wanders or if you don't have profound insights every time. The important thing is consistency.

5. Vary your approach: While it's good to have a consistent method, don't be afraid to vary your approach sometimes. You might try different meditation techniques, such as:

   - Lectio Divina: A traditional practice of scriptural reading, meditation, and prayer.
   - Verse mapping: Breaking down a verse word by word, exploring definitions and connections.
   - Imaginative meditation: Placing yourself in a Bible story and experiencing it through your senses.

6. Share with others: Consider joining a small group or finding a prayer partner to share your meditations with. This can provide accountability and enrich your understanding as you gain insights from others.

7. Be flexible: While consistency is important, don't become legalistic about your meditation practice. If you miss a day, simply start again the next day.

8. Create a meditation-friendly environment: Designate a specific place for your meditation time. This could be a comfortable chair, a quiet corner of your home, or even a spot in nature.

By following these steps and incorporating these tips, you can develop a rich and meaningful practice of meditating on God's Word. Remember, the goal is not perfection, but progress – growing closer to God and allowing His Word to transform you day by day.

New Age Meditation

New Age meditation has gained popularity in recent decades, often marketed as a secular practice for stress relief, self-improvement, and spiritual enlightenment. However, as Christians, it's crucial to understand that these practices often carry underlying philosophies and spiritual implications that can be at odds with our faith.

What is New Age Meditation?

New Age meditation encompasses a wide variety of practices, often borrowing from Eastern religions and philosophies. Some common forms include:

a) Transcendental Meditation: Involves the repetition of a mantra to achieve a state of relaxed awareness.

b) Mindfulness meditation: Focuses on being present in the moment and observing thoughts without judgment.

c) Guided visualizations: Uses mental imagery to achieve relaxation or manifest desired outcomes.

d) Energy healing meditations: Attempts to manipulate supposed energy fields in and around the body.

These practices often share common themes:

- The belief in an impersonal universal energy or life force
- The idea that individuals can tap into higher states of consciousness or realms of existence
- The concept of self-deification or the divinity of the self
- An emphasis on personal experience over objective truth
- The goal of self-realization or enlightenment through one's own efforts

While these ideas may seem harmless or even beneficial on the surface, they present significant spiritual challenges for Christians.

The Dangers of New Age Meditation for Christians

a) Spiritual deception:

New Age meditation often promotes the idea that truth is subjective and that one can find their own path to enlightenment. This contradicts the Christian belief in absolute truth and Jesus as the only way to God (John 14:6). Engaging in these practices may lead Christians to doubt the uniqueness of Christ and the authority of Scripture.

b) Opening oneself to spiritual influences:

Many New Age practices involve entering altered states of consciousness or inviting spiritual entities for guidance. From a Christian perspective, this can be dangerous, as it may open individuals to demonic influence. The Bible warns against engaging with spiritual forces outside of God (Deuteronomy 18:10-12).

c) Misplaced focus on self:

New Age meditation often emphasizes self-realization and personal power. This self-centered approach contrasts sharply with the Christian call to deny oneself and follow Christ (Luke 9:23). It can lead to pride and a diminished reliance on God's grace.

d) Blurred spiritual boundaries:

Participating in New Age meditation may gradually erode a Christian's spiritual discernment. As one becomes more accepting of these practices, it becomes easier to incorporate other non-Christian beliefs, leading to syncretism.

e) False sense of spiritual growth:

The relaxation and positive feelings often associated with meditation can be mistaken for genuine spiritual progress. This may cause Christians to neglect true spiritual disciplines and the pursuit of holiness through Christ.

f) Undermining the gospel:

New Age philosophy often teaches that humans are inherently divine and need only to realize their true nature. This directly contradicts the Christian understanding of sin, salvation, and the need for a Savior.

g) Ethical relativism:

Many New Age practices promote the idea that there is no absolute right or wrong, only personal truth. This can lead to moral confusion and a departure from biblical ethical standards.

h) Distraction from true spiritual warfare:

While New Age practices might promise spiritual power or protection, they distract from the true spiritual battle Christians face and the armour God provides (Ephesians 6:10-18).

Differences Between Christian and New Age Meditation

Understanding the distinctions between Christian meditation and New Age practices is crucial for maintaining a strong, biblically grounded faith:

a) Focus:

- Christian meditation: Centered on God's Word and character
- New Age meditation: Often focuses on self, cosmic energy, or emptying the mind

b) Purpose:

- Christian meditation: To know God more deeply, grow in faith, and align with His will
- New Age meditation: Self-improvement, achieving higher consciousness, or manipulating reality

c) Source of truth:

- Christian meditation: Relies on the Bible as the authoritative word of God
- New Age meditation: Often draws from various spiritual traditions or personal insight

d) View of self:

- Christian meditation: Recognizes human sinfulness and the need for redemption through Christ
- New Age meditation: Often promotes the idea of human divinity or innate perfection

e) Spiritual entities:

- Christian meditation: Engages with the Triune God through prayer and reflection
- New Age meditation: May involve contacting spirit guides, ascended masters, or impersonal forces

f) End goal:

- Christian meditation: Transformation into Christ-likeness and intimacy with God
- New Age meditation: Self-realization, enlightenment, or unity with the universe

g) Ethical framework:

- Christian meditation: Grounded in biblical morality and God's unchanging nature
- New Age meditation: Often promotes moral relativism or situational ethics

h) View of suffering:

- Christian meditation: Acknowledges the reality of suffering and sees it as an opportunity for growth and reliance on God
- New Age meditation: Often seeks to transcend or deny suffering through mental techniques

Responding to New Age Influences

As Christians, it's important to respond to the prevalence of New Age meditation with wisdom and grace:

- Educate yourself and others about the differences between Christian and New Age practices

- Be discerning about meditation techniques offered in secular settings (e.g., workplaces, schools)
- Offer Christian alternatives for stress relief and spiritual growth
- Engage in respectful dialogue with those involved in New Age practices, sharing the hope of the gospel
- Strengthen your own practice of biblical meditation and prayer

4

Conclusion

As we draw our exploration of Christian meditation to a close, it's essential to reflect on the profound insights and practical wisdom we've uncovered throughout this journey. We began by understanding the rich historical and linguistic roots of meditation within the Judeo-Christian tradition, discovering that this practice is far from a New Age concept or Eastern import. Rather, it is a fundamental aspect of our faith, deeply embedded in Scripture and the lives of countless believers who have gone before us.

The Hebrew words "hagah" and "siyach," which we have earlier talked about, revealed that meditation in the biblical context is not about emptying our minds, but rather filling them with God's truth. It's a process of rumination, of turning over Scripture in our minds like a cow chews its cud, extracting every last bit of spiritual nourishment. This understanding sets the stage for a uniquely Christian approach to meditation that is transformative and life-giving.

Throughout this book, we've emphasized that meditating on God's Word is not merely an intellectual exercise. It's a holistic practice that engages our mind, heart, and spirit in communion with the living God. By focusing our thoughts on Scripture, we open ourselves to the gentle yet powerful work of the Holy Spirit, who illuminates truth and applies it to our lives in ways that mere academic study cannot achieve.

We've explored the several benefits of this practice, from deeper spiritual insight and a more intimate relationship with God to practical advantages like reduced stress and improved mental clarity. Christian meditation offers a unique synthesis of spiritual growth and personal well-being, addressing the needs of our entire being in a way that aligns with God's design for human flourishing.

The step-by-step guide provided in this book offers a practical roadmap for incorporating meditation into your daily life. Remember, the goal is not perfection but persistence. Start small, perhaps with just a few minutes each day, and allow your practice to grow organically. As you make space in your life for this discipline, you'll likely find that it becomes not just a duty but a delight – a cherished time of connection with your Creator.

It's crucial to reiterate the distinction between Christian meditation and its New Age counterparts. While there may be surface-level similarities, the core purposes and spiritual foundations are fundamentally different. Christian meditation is always centered on God and His Word, not on self or an impersonal cosmic force. It's about aligning our thoughts with divine truth, not emptying our minds or seeking altered states of consciousness.

As you move forward from this book, I encourage you to view Christian meditation not as another task on your spiritual to-do list, but as an invitation to a deeper, richer experience of faith. It's an opportunity to slow down in our fast-paced world and truly listen to the voice of God speaking through His Word. In a culture that constantly bombards us with noise and distraction, cultivating this practice of intentional, focused reflection on Scripture can be revolutionary.

Remember, too, that Christian meditation is not meant to be practiced in isolation. Share what you're learning with fellow believers. Consider starting a small group where you can meditate on Scripture together, discussing your insights and encouraging one another in this discipline. The body of Christ grows stronger when we share our spiritual practices and learn from one another.

As you embark on or continue your journey of Christian meditation, be patient with yourself. Like any worthwhile skill, it takes time to develop. There may be days when your mind wanders or when the insights don't seem to flow. This is normal and part of the process. The key is to persevere, trusting that God honours our sincere efforts to draw near to Him.

Finally, let this practice of meditation spill over into every aspect of your life. As you become more attuned to God's voice through Scripture, you'll likely find yourself more aware of His presence throughout your day. The truths you meditate on in your quiet time will resurface in moments of decision, hardship, or joy, providing guidance, comfort, and reason for praise.

Christian meditation is a powerful tool for spiritual growth, a time-honored practice rooted in Scripture, and a means of deepening our relationship with God. It offers a counter-cultural approach to the busyness and distraction of modern life, inviting us into a space of quiet reflection and divine encounter. As you close this book, my hope is that you'll open your heart to this transformative practice, allowing the Word of God to dwell in you richly, shaping your thoughts, guiding your actions, and drawing you ever closer to the heart of your loving Creator.

May your journey of Christian meditation be filled with profound discoveries, moments of divine insight, and a growing sense of God's presence in your daily life. Remember, every moment spent meditating on God's Word is an investment in your spiritual growth and a step towards a more vibrant, purposeful faith. Embrace this practice with joy and expectation, knowing that as you seek God through His Word, He will faithfully reveal Himself to you in ever-deepening ways.

WHAT IS GOD SAYING TODAY?

SCRIPTURE ON WHICH TO MEDITATE:

Proverbs 3:6 ESV

"In all your ways acknowledge him, and he will make straight your paths."

NOTE DISTRACTIONS & REMINDERS:

THOUGHTS, PICTURES, WORDS, OR SONGS THAT COME TO MIND:

ACTIONS TO TAKE:

WHAT IS GOD SAYING TODAY?

SCRIPTURE ON WHICH TO MEDITATE:

NOTE DISTRACTIONS & REMINDERS:

Romans 10:17 ESV
"So faith comes from hearing, and hearing through the word of Christ."

THOUGHTS, PICTURES, WORDS, OR SONGS THAT COME TO MIND:

ACTIONS TO TAKE:

WHAT IS GOD SAYING TODAY?

SCRIPTURE ON WHICH TO MEDITATE:

John 6:63 ESV
"It is the Spirit who gives life; the flesh is no help at all. The words that I have spoken to you are spirit and life."

NOTE DISTRACTIONS & REMINDERS:

THOUGHTS, PICTURES, WORDS, OR SONGS THAT COME TO MIND:

ACTIONS TO TAKE:

WHAT IS GOD SAYING TODAY?

SCRIPTURE ON WHICH TO MEDITATE:

John 14:26 ESV
"But the Helper, the Holy Spirit, whom the Father will send in my name, he will teach you all things and bring to your remembrance all that I have said to you."

NOTE DISTRACTIONS & REMINDERS:

THOUGHTS, PICTURES, WORDS, OR SONGS THAT COME TO MIND:

ACTIONS TO TAKE:

WHAT IS GOD SAYING TODAY?

SCRIPTURE ON WHICH TO MEDITATE:

Revelation 3:20 ESV
"Behold, I stand at the door and knock. If anyone hears my voice and opens the door, I will come in to him and eat with him, and he with me."

NOTE DISTRACTIONS & REMINDERS:

THOUGHTS, PICTURES, WORDS, OR SONGS THAT COME TO MIND:

ACTIONS TO TAKE:

SCRIPTURE ON WHICH TO MEDITATE:

Jeremiah 33:3 ESV
"Call to me and I will answer you, and will tell you great and hidden things that you have not known."

NOTE DISTRACTIONS & REMINDERS:

THOUGHTS, PICTURES, WORDS, OR SONGS THAT COME TO MIND:

ACTIONS TO TAKE:

SCRIPTURE ON WHICH TO MEDITATE:

Ezekiel 43:2 ESV
"And behold, the glory of the God of Israel was coming from the east. And the sound of his coming was like the sound of many waters, and the earth shone with his glory."

NOTE DISTRACTIONS & REMINDERS:

THOUGHTS, PICTURES, WORDS, OR SONGS THAT COME TO MIND:

ACTIONS TO TAKE:

WHAT IS GOD SAYING TODAY?

SCRIPTURE ON WHICH TO MEDITATE:

Luke 11:28 ESV

"Blessed rather are those who hear the word of God and keep it!"

NOTE DISTRACTIONS & REMINDERS:

THOUGHTS, PICTURES, WORDS, OR SONGS THAT COME TO MIND:

ACTIONS TO TAKE:

WHAT IS GOD SAYING TODAY?

SCRIPTURE ON WHICH TO MEDITATE:

Psalm 119:105 ESV
"Your word is a lamp to my feet and a light to my path."

NOTE DISTRACTIONS & REMINDERS:

THOUGHTS, PICTURES, WORDS, OR SONGS THAT COME TO MIND:

ACTIONS TO TAKE:

SCRIPTURE ON WHICH TO MEDITATE:

John 16:13 ESV

"When the Spirit of truth comes, he will guide you into all the truth, for he will not speak on his own authority, but whatever he hears he will speak, and he will declare to you the things that are to come."

NOTE DISTRACTIONS & REMINDERS:

THOUGHTS, PICTURES, WORDS, OR SONGS THAT COME TO MIND:

ACTIONS TO TAKE:

WHAT IS GOD SAYING TODAY?

SCRIPTURE ON WHICH TO MEDITATE:

Romans 8:14 ESV
"For all who are led by the Spirit of God are sons of God."

NOTE DISTRACTIONS & REMINDERS:

THOUGHTS, PICTURES, WORDS, OR SONGS THAT COME TO MIND:

ACTIONS TO TAKE:

WHAT IS GOD SAYING TODAY?

SCRIPTURE ON WHICH TO MEDITATE:

John 10:16 ESV
"And I have other sheep that are not of this fold. I must bring them also, and they will listen to my voice. So there will be one flock, one shepherd."

NOTE DISTRACTIONS & REMINDERS:

THOUGHTS, PICTURES, WORDS, OR SONGS THAT COME TO MIND:

ACTIONS TO TAKE:

WHAT IS GOD SAYING TODAY?

SCRIPTURE ON WHICH TO MEDITATE:

Hebrews 2:1 ESV

"Therefore we must pay much closer attention to what we have heard, lest we drift away from it."

NOTE DISTRACTIONS & REMINDERS:

THOUGHTS, PICTURES, WORDS, OR SONGS THAT COME TO MIND:

ACTIONS TO TAKE:

SCRIPTURE ON WHICH TO MEDITATE:

Hebrews 3:15 ESV

"Today, if you hear his voice, do not harden your hearts as in the rebellion."

NOTE DISTRACTIONS & REMINDERS:

THOUGHTS, PICTURES, WORDS, OR SONGS THAT COME TO MIND:

ACTIONS TO TAKE:

WHAT IS GOD SAYING TODAY?

SCRIPTURE ON WHICH TO MEDITATE:

John 10:27-28 ESV

"My sheep hear my voice, and I know them, and they follow me. I give them eternal life, and they will never perish, and no one will snatch them out of my hand."

NOTE DISTRACTIONS & REMINDERS:

THOUGHTS, PICTURES, WORDS, OR SONGS THAT COME TO MIND:

ACTIONS TO TAKE:

WHAT IS GOD SAYING TODAY?

SCRIPTURE ON WHICH TO MEDITATE:

John 1:1 ESV

"In the beginning was the Word, and the Word was with God, and the Word was God."

NOTE DISTRACTIONS & REMINDERS:

THOUGHTS, PICTURES, WORDS, OR SONGS THAT COME TO MIND:

ACTIONS TO TAKE:

WHAT IS GOD SAYING TODAY?

SCRIPTURE ON WHICH TO MEDITATE:

Jeremiah 29:13 ESV
"You will seek me and find me, when you seek me with all your heart."

NOTE DISTRACTIONS & REMINDERS:

THOUGHTS, PICTURES, WORDS, OR SONGS THAT COME TO MIND:

ACTIONS TO TAKE:

DATE: # WHAT IS GOD SAYING TODAY? 

SCRIPTURE ON WHICH TO MEDITATE:

Deuteronomy 13:4 ESV
"You shall walk after the Lord your God and fear him and keep his commandments and obey his voice, and you shall serve him and hold fast to him."

NOTE DISTRACTIONS & REMINDERS:

THOUGHTS, PICTURES, WORDS, OR SONGS THAT COME TO MIND:

ACTIONS TO TAKE:

WHAT IS GOD SAYING TODAY?

SCRIPTURE ON WHICH TO MEDITATE:

GALATIANS 5:25

"If we live by the Spirit, let us also keep in step with the Spirit."

NOTE DISTRACTIONS & REMINDERS:

THOUGHTS, PICTURES, WORDS, OR SONGS THAT COME TO MIND:

ACTIONS TO TAKE:

WHAT IS GOD SAYING TODAY?

SCRIPTURE ON WHICH TO MEDITATE:

John 4:24

"God is spirit, and those who worship him must worship in spirit and truth."

NOTE DISTRACTIONS & REMINDERS:

THOUGHTS, PICTURES, WORDS, OR SONGS THAT COME TO MIND:

ACTIONS TO TAKE:

WHAT IS GOD SAYING TODAY?

SCRIPTURE ON WHICH TO MEDITATE:

John 16:13 ESV

"When the Spirit of truth comes, he will guide you into all the truth, for he will not speak on his own authority, but whatever he hears he will speak, and he will declare to you the things that are to come."

NOTE DISTRACTIONS & REMINDERS:

THOUGHTS, PICTURES, WORDS, OR SONGS THAT COME TO MIND:

ACTIONS TO TAKE:

SCRIPTURE ON WHICH TO MEDITATE:

Psalm 32:8 ESV

"I will instruct you and teach you in the way you should go; I will counsel you with my eye upon you."

NOTE DISTRACTIONS & REMINDERS:

THOUGHTS, PICTURES, WORDS, OR SONGS THAT COME TO MIND:

ACTIONS TO TAKE:

WHAT IS GOD SAYING TODAY? 

SCRIPTURE ON WHICH TO MEDITATE:

Revelation 4:1 ESV

"After this I looked, and behold, a door standing open in heaven! And the first voice, which I had heard speaking to me like a trumpet, said, "Come up here, and I will show you what must take place after this."

NOTE DISTRACTIONS & REMINDERS:

THOUGHTS, PICTURES, WORDS, OR SONGS THAT COME TO MIND:

ACTIONS TO TAKE:

SCRIPTURE ON WHICH TO MEDITATE:

Psalm 46:10 ESV
"Be still, and know that I am God. I will be exalted among the nations, I will be exalted in the earth!" text

NOTE DISTRACTIONS & REMINDERS:

THOUGHTS, PICTURES, WORDS, OR SONGS THAT COME TO MIND:

ACTIONS TO TAKE:

WHAT IS GOD SAYING TODAY?

SCRIPTURE ON WHICH TO MEDITATE:

Revelation 3:11 ESV
"I am coming soon. Hold fast what you have, so that no one may seize your crown."

NOTE DISTRACTIONS & REMINDERS:

THOUGHTS, PICTURES, WORDS, OR SONGS THAT COME TO MIND:

ACTIONS TO TAKE:

WHAT IS GOD SAYING TODAY?

SCRIPTURE ON WHICH TO MEDITATE:

Galatians 5:16 ESV
"But I say, walk by the Spirit, and you will not gratify the desires of the flesh."

NOTE DISTRACTIONS & REMINDERS:

THOUGHTS, PICTURES, WORDS, OR SONGS THAT COME TO MIND:

ACTIONS TO TAKE:

WHAT IS GOD SAYING TODAY?

SCRIPTURE ON WHICH TO MEDITATE:

Romans 8:26 ESV
Likewise the Spirit helps us in our weakness. For we do not know what to pray for as we ought, but the Spirit himself intercedes for us with groanings too deep for words.

NOTE DISTRACTIONS & REMINDERS:

THOUGHTS, PICTURES, WORDS, OR SONGS THAT COME TO MIND:

ACTIONS TO TAKE:

WHAT IS GOD SAYING TODAY?

SCRIPTURE ON WHICH TO MEDITATE:

Romans 8:5 ESV

For those who live according to the flesh set their minds on the things of the flesh, but those who live according to the Spirit set their minds on the things of the Spirit.

NOTE DISTRACTIONS & REMINDERS:

THOUGHTS, PICTURES, WORDS, OR SONGS THAT COME TO MIND:

ACTIONS TO TAKE:

WHAT IS GOD SAYING TODAY?

SCRIPTURE ON WHICH TO MEDITATE:

2 Peter 1:21 ESV
"For no prophecy was ever produced by the will of man, but men spoke from God as they were carried along by the Holy Spirit."

NOTE DISTRACTIONS & REMINDERS:

THOUGHTS, PICTURES, WORDS, OR SONGS THAT COME TO MIND:

ACTIONS TO TAKE:

SCRIPTURE ON WHICH TO MEDITATE:

2 Timothy 1:7 ESV
"For God gave us a spirit not of fear but of power and love and self-control."

NOTE DISTRACTIONS & REMINDERS:

THOUGHTS, PICTURES, WORDS, OR SONGS THAT COME TO MIND:

ACTIONS TO TAKE:

WHAT IS GOD SAYING TODAY?

SCRIPTURE ON WHICH TO MEDITATE:

Romans 12:2 ESV

"Do not be conformed to this world, but be transformed by the renewal of your mind, that by testing you may discern what is the will of God, what is good and acceptable and perfect."

NOTE DISTRACTIONS & REMINDERS:

THOUGHTS, PICTURES, WORDS, OR SONGS THAT COME TO MIND:

ACTIONS TO TAKE:

WHAT IS GOD SAYING TODAY?

SCRIPTURE ON WHICH TO MEDITATE:

Ephesians 4:30 ESV

"And do not grieve the Holy Spirit of God, by whom you were sealed for the day of redemption."

NOTE DISTRACTIONS & REMINDERS:

THOUGHTS, PICTURES, WORDS, OR SONGS THAT COME TO MIND:

ACTIONS TO TAKE:

SCRIPTURE ON WHICH TO MEDITATE:

1 Corinthians 12:13 ESV
"For in one Spirit we were all baptized into one body—Jews or Greeks, slaves or free—and all were made to drink of one Spirit."

NOTE DISTRACTIONS & REMINDERS:

THOUGHTS, PICTURES, WORDS, OR SONGS THAT COME TO MIND:

ACTIONS TO TAKE:

WHAT IS GOD SAYING TODAY?

SCRIPTURE ON WHICH TO MEDITATE:

Romans 8:13 ESV

"For if you live according to the flesh you will die, but if by the Spirit you put to death the deeds of the body, you will live."

NOTE DISTRACTIONS & REMINDERS:

THOUGHTS, PICTURES, WORDS, OR SONGS THAT COME TO MIND:

ACTIONS TO TAKE:

WHAT IS GOD SAYING TODAY?

SCRIPTURE ON WHICH TO MEDITATE:

Galatians 4:6 ESV
"And because you are sons, God has sent the Spirit of his Son into our hearts, crying, "Abba! Father!"

NOTE DISTRACTIONS & REMINDERS:

THOUGHTS, PICTURES, WORDS, OR SONGS THAT COME TO MIND:

ACTIONS TO TAKE:

WHAT IS GOD SAYING TODAY?

SCRIPTURE ON WHICH TO MEDITATE:

Matthew 28:19 ESV

"Go therefore and make disciples of all nations, baptizing them in the name of the Father and of the Son and of the Holy Spirit,"

NOTE DISTRACTIONS & REMINDERS:

THOUGHTS, PICTURES, WORDS, OR SONGS THAT COME TO MIND:

ACTIONS TO TAKE:

WHAT IS GOD SAYING TODAY?

SCRIPTURE ON WHICH TO MEDITATE:

Romans 8:6 ESV

"For to set the mind on the flesh is death, but to set the mind on the Spirit is life and peace."

NOTE DISTRACTIONS & REMINDERS:

THOUGHTS, PICTURES, WORDS, OR SONGS THAT COME TO MIND:

ACTIONS TO TAKE:

WHAT IS GOD SAYING TODAY?

SCRIPTURE ON WHICH TO MEDITATE:

Romans 8:15 ESV
"For you did not receive the spirit of slavery to fall back into fear, but you have received the Spirit of adoption as sons, by whom we cry, "Abba! Father!"

NOTE DISTRACTIONS & REMINDERS:

THOUGHTS, PICTURES, WORDS, OR SONGS THAT COME TO MIND:

ACTIONS TO TAKE:

WHAT IS GOD SAYING TODAY?

SCRIPTURE ON WHICH TO MEDITATE:

Psalm 143:10 ESV

"Teach me to do your will, for you are my God! Let your good Spirit lead me on level ground!"

NOTE DISTRACTIONS & REMINDERS:

THOUGHTS, PICTURES, WORDS, OR SONGS THAT COME TO MIND:

ACTIONS TO TAKE:

WHAT IS GOD SAYING TODAY?

SCRIPTURE ON WHICH TO MEDITATE:

1 Corinthians 2:14 ESV
"The natural person does not accept the things of the Spirit of God, for they are folly to him, and he is not able to understand them because they are spiritually discerned."

NOTE DISTRACTIONS & REMINDERS:

THOUGHTS, PICTURES, WORDS, OR SONGS THAT COME TO MIND:

ACTIONS TO TAKE:

WHAT IS GOD SAYING TODAY?

SCRIPTURE ON WHICH TO MEDITATE:

Romans 8:2 ESV

"For the law of the Spirit of life has set you free in Christ Jesus from the law of sin and death."

NOTE DISTRACTIONS & REMINDERS:

THOUGHTS, PICTURES, WORDS, OR SONGS THAT COME TO MIND:

ACTIONS TO TAKE:

WHAT IS GOD SAYING TODAY?

SCRIPTURE ON WHICH TO MEDITATE:

Romans 5:5 ESV

"And hope does not put us to shame, because God's love has been poured into our hearts through the Holy Spirit who has been given to us."

NOTE DISTRACTIONS & REMINDERS:

THOUGHTS, PICTURES, WORDS, OR SONGS THAT COME TO MIND:

ACTIONS TO TAKE:

WHAT IS GOD SAYING TODAY?

SCRIPTURE ON WHICH TO MEDITATE:

1 Peter 4:10 ESV

"As each has received a gift, use it to serve one another, as good stewards of God's varied grace."

NOTE DISTRACTIONS & REMINDERS:

THOUGHTS, PICTURES, WORDS, OR SONGS THAT COME TO MIND:

ACTIONS TO TAKE:

WHAT IS GOD SAYING TODAY?

SCRIPTURE ON WHICH TO MEDITATE:

1 Corinthians 2:13 ESV
"And we impart this in words not taught by human wisdom but taught by the Spirit, interpreting spiritual truths to those who are spiritual."

NOTE DISTRACTIONS & REMINDERS:

THOUGHTS, PICTURES, WORDS, OR SONGS THAT COME TO MIND:

ACTIONS TO TAKE:

WHAT IS GOD SAYING TODAY?

SCRIPTURE ON WHICH TO MEDITATE:

1 Corinthians 2:13 ESV
"And we impart this in words not taught by human wisdom but taught by the Spirit, interpreting spiritual truths to those who are spiritual."

NOTE DISTRACTIONS & REMINDERS:

THOUGHTS, PICTURES, WORDS, OR SONGS THAT COME TO MIND:

ACTIONS TO TAKE:

WHAT IS GOD SAYING TODAY?

SCRIPTURE ON WHICH TO MEDITATE:

Ephesians 3:16-17 ESV

"That according to the riches of his glory he may grant you to be strengthened with power through his Spirit in your inner being, so that Christ may dwell in your hearts through faith— that you, being rooted and grounded in love,"

NOTE DISTRACTIONS & REMINDERS:

THOUGHTS, PICTURES, WORDS, OR SONGS THAT COME TO MIND:

ACTIONS TO TAKE:

WHAT IS GOD SAYING TODAY?

SCRIPTURE ON WHICH TO MEDITATE:

2 Corinthians 3:18 ESV

"And we all, with unveiled face, beholding the glory of the Lord, are being transformed into the same image from one degree of glory to another. For this comes from the Lord who is the Spirit".

NOTE DISTRACTIONS & REMINDERS:

THOUGHTS, PICTURES, WORDS, OR SONGS THAT COME TO MIND:

ACTIONS TO TAKE:

SCRIPTURE ON WHICH TO MEDITATE:

Romans 6:14 ESV
"For sin will have no dominion over you, since you are not under law but under grace."

NOTE DISTRACTIONS & REMINDERS:

THOUGHTS, PICTURES, WORDS, OR SONGS THAT COME TO MIND:

ACTIONS TO TAKE:

WHAT IS GOD SAYING TODAY?

SCRIPTURE ON WHICH TO MEDITATE:

Ephesians 1:13 ESV
"In him you also, when you heard the word of truth, the gospel of your salvation, and believed in him, were sealed with the promised Holy Spirit."

NOTE DISTRACTIONS & REMINDERS:

THOUGHTS, PICTURES, WORDS, OR SONGS THAT COME TO MIND:

ACTIONS TO TAKE:

WHAT IS GOD SAYING TODAY?

SCRIPTURE ON WHICH TO MEDITATE:

Romans 6:14 ESV

"For sin will have no dominion over you, since you are not under law but under grace."

NOTE DISTRACTIONS & REMINDERS:

THOUGHTS, PICTURES, WORDS, OR SONGS THAT COME TO MIND:

ACTIONS TO TAKE:

WHAT IS GOD SAYING TODAY?

SCRIPTURE ON WHICH TO MEDITATE:

Isaiah 61:1 ESV

"The Spirit of the Lord God is upon me, because the Lord has anointed me to bring good news to the poor; he has sent me to bind up the brokenhearted, to proclaim liberty to the captives, and the opening of the prison to those who are bound."

NOTE DISTRACTIONS & REMINDERS:

THOUGHTS, PICTURES, WORDS, OR SONGS THAT COME TO MIND:

ACTIONS TO TAKE:

WHAT IS GOD SAYING TODAY?

SCRIPTURE ON WHICH TO MEDITATE:

Galatians 4:5 ESV

"To redeem those who were under the law, so that we might receive adoption as sons."

NOTE DISTRACTIONS & REMINDERS:

THOUGHTS, PICTURES, WORDS, OR SONGS THAT COME TO MIND:

ACTIONS TO TAKE:

WHAT IS GOD SAYING TODAY?

SCRIPTURE ON WHICH TO MEDITATE:

Romans 8:11 ESV

"If the Spirit of him who raised Jesus from the dead dwells in you, he who raised Christ Jesus from the dead will also give life to your mortal bodies through his Spirit who dwells in you."

NOTE DISTRACTIONS & REMINDERS:

THOUGHTS, PICTURES, WORDS, OR SONGS THAT COME TO MIND:

ACTIONS TO TAKE:

WHAT IS GOD SAYING TODAY?

SCRIPTURE ON WHICH TO MEDITATE:

Romans 14:17 ESV
"For the kingdom of God is not a matter of eating and drinking but of righteousness and peace and joy in the Holy Spirit."

NOTE DISTRACTIONS & REMINDERS:

THOUGHTS, PICTURES, WORDS, OR SONGS THAT COME TO MIND:

ACTIONS TO TAKE:

WHAT IS GOD SAYING TODAY?

SCRIPTURE ON WHICH TO MEDITATE:

Romans 8:7 ESV

For the mind that is set on the flesh is hostile to God, for it does not submit to God's law; indeed, it cannot.

NOTE DISTRACTIONS & REMINDERS:

THOUGHTS, PICTURES, WORDS, OR SONGS THAT COME TO MIND:

ACTIONS TO TAKE:

WHAT IS GOD SAYING TODAY?

SCRIPTURE ON WHICH TO MEDITATE:

Proverbs 20:27 ESV
The spirit of man is the lamp of the Lord, searching all his innermost parts.

NOTE DISTRACTIONS & REMINDERS:

THOUGHTS, PICTURES, WORDS, OR SONGS THAT COME TO MIND:

ACTIONS TO TAKE:

WHAT IS GOD SAYING TODAY?

SCRIPTURE ON WHICH TO MEDITATE:

Acts 2:4 ESV
And they were all filled with the Holy Spirit and began to speak in other tongues as the Spirit gave them utterance.

NOTE DISTRACTIONS & REMINDERS:

THOUGHTS, PICTURES, WORDS, OR SONGS THAT COME TO MIND:

ACTIONS TO TAKE:

WHAT IS GOD SAYING TODAY?

SCRIPTURE ON WHICH TO MEDITATE:

Ephesians 2:10 ESV
"For we are his workmanship, created in Christ Jesus for good works, which God prepared beforehand, that we should walk in them."

NOTE DISTRACTIONS & REMINDERS:

THOUGHTS, PICTURES, WORDS, OR SONGS THAT COME TO MIND:

ACTIONS TO TAKE:

SCRIPTURE ON WHICH TO MEDITATE:

James 1:5 ESV

"If any of you lacks wisdom, let him ask God, who gives generously to all without reproach, and it will be given him."

NOTE DISTRACTIONS & REMINDERS:

THOUGHTS, PICTURES, WORDS, OR SONGS THAT COME TO MIND:

ACTIONS TO TAKE:

WHAT IS GOD SAYING TODAY?

SCRIPTURE ON WHICH TO MEDITATE:

Proverbs 1:7 ESV

"The fear of the Lord is the beginning of knowledge; fools despise wisdom and instruction."

NOTE DISTRACTIONS & REMINDERS:

THOUGHTS, PICTURES, WORDS, OR SONGS THAT COME TO MIND:

ACTIONS TO TAKE:

WHAT IS GOD SAYING TODAY?

SCRIPTURE ON WHICH TO MEDITATE:

1 Corinthians 2:10 ESV
"These things God has revealed to us through the Spirit. For the Spirit searches everything, even the depths of God."

NOTE DISTRACTIONS & REMINDERS:

THOUGHTS, PICTURES, WORDS, OR SONGS THAT COME TO MIND:

ACTIONS TO TAKE:

WHAT IS GOD SAYING TODAY?

SCRIPTURE ON WHICH TO MEDITATE:

John 14:6 ESV

"Jesus said to him, "I am the way, and the truth, and the life. No one comes to the Father except through me."

NOTE DISTRACTIONS & REMINDERS:

THOUGHTS, PICTURES, WORDS, OR SONGS THAT COME TO MIND:

ACTIONS TO TAKE:

WHAT IS GOD SAYING TODAY?

SCRIPTURE ON WHICH TO MEDITATE:

John 1:1 ESV

"In the beginning was the Word, and the Word was with God, and the Word was God."

NOTE DISTRACTIONS & REMINDERS:

THOUGHTS, PICTURES, WORDS, OR SONGS THAT COME TO MIND:

ACTIONS TO TAKE:

WHAT IS GOD SAYING TODAY?

SCRIPTURE ON WHICH TO MEDITATE:

Romans 12:11 ESV
"Do not be slothful in zeal, be fervent in spirit, serve the Lord."

NOTE DISTRACTIONS & REMINDERS:

THOUGHTS, PICTURES, WORDS, OR SONGS THAT COME TO MIND:

ACTIONS TO TAKE:

WHAT IS GOD SAYING TODAY?

SCRIPTURE ON WHICH TO MEDITATE:

Matthew 26:41 ESV
"Watch and pray that you may not enter into temptation. The spirit indeed is willing, but the flesh is weak."

NOTE DISTRACTIONS & REMINDERS:

THOUGHTS, PICTURES, WORDS, OR SONGS THAT COME TO MIND:

ACTIONS TO TAKE:

SCRIPTURE ON WHICH TO MEDITATE:

Isaiah 11:2 ESV
"And the Spirit of the Lord shall rest upon him, the Spirit of wisdom and understanding, the Spirit of counsel and might, the Spirit of knowledge and the fear of the Lord."

NOTE DISTRACTIONS & REMINDERS:

THOUGHTS, PICTURES, WORDS, OR SONGS THAT COME TO MIND:

ACTIONS TO TAKE:

WHAT IS GOD SAYING TODAY?

SCRIPTURE ON WHICH TO MEDITATE:

Proverbs 19:8 ESV

"Whoever gets sense loves his own soul; he who keeps understanding will discover good."

NOTE DISTRACTIONS & REMINDERS:

THOUGHTS, PICTURES, WORDS, OR SONGS THAT COME TO MIND:

ACTIONS TO TAKE:

SCRIPTURE ON WHICH TO MEDITATE:

2 Timothy 3:16 ESV
"All Scripture is breathed out by God and profitable for teaching, for reproof, for correction, and for training in righteousness."

NOTE DISTRACTIONS & REMINDERS:

THOUGHTS, PICTURES, WORDS, OR SONGS THAT COME TO MIND:

ACTIONS TO TAKE:

WHAT IS GOD SAYING TODAY? 

SCRIPTURE ON WHICH TO MEDITATE:

Revelation 3:20 ESV
"Behold, I stand at the door and knock. If anyone hears my voice and opens the door, I will come in to him and eat with him, and he with me."

NOTE DISTRACTIONS & REMINDERS:

THOUGHTS, PICTURES, WORDS, OR SONGS THAT COME TO MIND:

ACTIONS TO TAKE:

WHAT IS GOD SAYING TODAY?

SCRIPTURE ON WHICH TO MEDITATE:

Isaiah 30:21 ESV

"And your ears shall hear a word behind you, saying, "This is the way, walk in it," when you turn to the right or when you turn to the left."

NOTE DISTRACTIONS & REMINDERS:

THOUGHTS, PICTURES, WORDS, OR SONGS THAT COME TO MIND:

ACTIONS TO TAKE:

WHAT IS GOD SAYING TODAY?

SCRIPTURE ON WHICH TO MEDITATE:

John 10:27 ESV

"My sheep hear my voice, and I know them, and they follow me."

NOTE DISTRACTIONS & REMINDERS:

THOUGHTS, PICTURES, WORDS, OR SONGS THAT COME TO MIND:

ACTIONS TO TAKE:

WHAT IS GOD SAYING TODAY?

SCRIPTURE ON WHICH TO MEDITATE:

Psalm 25:4 ESV

"Make me to know your ways, O Lord; teach me your paths."

NOTE DISTRACTIONS & REMINDERS:

THOUGHTS, PICTURES, WORDS, OR SONGS THAT COME TO MIND:

ACTIONS TO TAKE:

WHAT IS GOD SAYING TODAY?

SCRIPTURE ON WHICH TO MEDITATE:

Proverbs 4:7 ESV
"The beginning of wisdom is this: Get wisdom, and whatever you get, get insight."

NOTE DISTRACTIONS & REMINDERS:

THOUGHTS, PICTURES, WORDS, OR SONGS THAT COME TO MIND:

ACTIONS TO TAKE:

SCRIPTURE ON WHICH TO MEDITATE:

Romans 11:33 ESV
"Oh, the depth of the riches and wisdom and knowledge of God! How unsearchable are his judgments and how inscrutable his ways!"

NOTE DISTRACTIONS & REMINDERS:

THOUGHTS, PICTURES, WORDS, OR SONGS THAT COME TO MIND:

ACTIONS TO TAKE:

WHAT IS GOD SAYING TODAY?

SCRIPTURE ON WHICH TO MEDITATE:

Colossians 4:5-6 ESV

"Walk in wisdom toward outsiders, making the best use of the time. Let your speech always be gracious, seasoned with salt, so that you may know how you ought to answer each person."

NOTE DISTRACTIONS & REMINDERS:

THOUGHTS, PICTURES, WORDS, OR SONGS THAT COME TO MIND:

ACTIONS TO TAKE:

WHAT IS GOD SAYING TODAY?

SCRIPTURE ON WHICH TO MEDITATE:

Proverbs 3:7 ESV
"Be not wise in your own eyes; fear the Lord, and turn away from evil."

NOTE DISTRACTIONS & REMINDERS:

THOUGHTS, PICTURES, WORDS, OR SONGS THAT COME TO MIND:

ACTIONS TO TAKE:

WHAT IS GOD SAYING TODAY?

SCRIPTURE ON WHICH TO MEDITATE:

Psalm 119:66 ESV

"Teach me good judgment and knowledge, for I believe in your commandments."

NOTE DISTRACTIONS & REMINDERS:

THOUGHTS, PICTURES, WORDS, OR SONGS THAT COME TO MIND:

ACTIONS TO TAKE:

WHAT IS GOD SAYING TODAY?

SCRIPTURE ON WHICH TO MEDITATE:

Proverbs 8:35 ESV
"For whoever finds me finds life and obtains favor from the Lord."

NOTE DISTRACTIONS & REMINDERS:

THOUGHTS, PICTURES, WORDS, OR SONGS THAT COME TO MIND:

ACTIONS TO TAKE:

WHAT IS GOD SAYING TODAY?

SCRIPTURE ON WHICH TO MEDITATE:

Proverbs 29:11 ESV
"A fool gives full vent to his spirit, but a wise man quietly holds it back."

NOTE DISTRACTIONS & REMINDERS:

THOUGHTS, PICTURES, WORDS, OR SONGS THAT COME TO MIND:

ACTIONS TO TAKE:

WHAT IS GOD SAYING TODAY?

SCRIPTURE ON WHICH TO MEDITATE:

Revelation 1:8 ESV

"I am the Alpha and the Omega," says the Lord God, "who is and who was and who is to come, the Almighty."

NOTE DISTRACTIONS & REMINDERS:

THOUGHTS, PICTURES, WORDS, OR SONGS THAT COME TO MIND:

ACTIONS TO TAKE:

SCRIPTURE ON WHICH TO MEDITATE:

1 Corinthians 3:18 ESV
"Let no one deceive himself. If anyone among you thinks that he is wise in this age, let him become a fool that he may become wise."

NOTE DISTRACTIONS & REMINDERS:

THOUGHTS, PICTURES, WORDS, OR SONGS THAT COME TO MIND:

ACTIONS TO TAKE:

SCRIPTURE ON WHICH TO MEDITATE:

Isaiah 28:29 ESV
"This also comes from the Lord of hosts; he is wonderful in counsel and excellent in wisdom."

NOTE DISTRACTIONS & REMINDERS:

THOUGHTS, PICTURES, WORDS, OR SONGS THAT COME TO MIND:

ACTIONS TO TAKE:

SCRIPTURE ON WHICH TO MEDITATE:

Proverbs 4:5 ESV

"Get wisdom; get insight; do not forget, and do not turn away from the words of my mouth."

NOTE DISTRACTIONS & REMINDERS:

THOUGHTS, PICTURES, WORDS, OR SONGS THAT COME TO MIND:

ACTIONS TO TAKE:

WHAT IS GOD SAYING TODAY?

SCRIPTURE ON WHICH TO MEDITATE:

Revelation 21:5 ESV

" And he who was seated on the throne said, "Behold, I am making all things new." Also he said, "Write this down, for these words are trustworthy and true."

NOTE DISTRACTIONS & REMINDERS:

THOUGHTS, PICTURES, WORDS, OR SONGS THAT COME TO MIND:

ACTIONS TO TAKE:

WHAT IS GOD SAYING TODAY?

SCRIPTURE ON WHICH TO MEDITATE:

Hebrews 11:6 ESV
"And without faith it is impossible to please him, for whoever would draw near to God must believe that he exists and that he rewards those who seek him."

NOTE DISTRACTIONS & REMINDERS:

THOUGHTS, PICTURES, WORDS, OR SONGS THAT COME TO MIND:

ACTIONS TO TAKE:

WHAT IS GOD SAYING TODAY?

SCRIPTURE ON WHICH TO MEDITATE:

James 1:2 ESV

"Count it all joy, my brothers, when you meet trials of various kinds"

NOTE DISTRACTIONS & REMINDERS:

THOUGHTS, PICTURES, WORDS, OR SONGS THAT COME TO MIND:

ACTIONS TO TAKE:

WHAT IS GOD SAYING TODAY?

SCRIPTURE ON WHICH TO MEDITATE:

Hebrews 11:6 ESV
"And without faith it is impossible to please him, for whoever would draw near to God must believe that he exists and that he rewards those who seek him."

NOTE DISTRACTIONS & REMINDERS:

THOUGHTS, PICTURES, WORDS, OR SONGS THAT COME TO MIND:

ACTIONS TO TAKE:

WHAT IS GOD SAYING TODAY?

SCRIPTURE ON WHICH TO MEDITATE:

1 John 4:1 ESV

"Beloved, do not believe every spirit, but test the spirits to see whether they are from God, for many false prophets have gone out into the world."

NOTE DISTRACTIONS & REMINDERS:

THOUGHTS, PICTURES, WORDS, OR SONGS THAT COME TO MIND:

ACTIONS TO TAKE:

WHAT IS GOD SAYING TODAY?

SCRIPTURE ON WHICH TO MEDITATE:

Y1 Corinthians 2:9-10
ESV

"What no eye has seen, nor ear heard, nor the heart of man imagined, what God has prepared for those who love him"— these things God has revealed to us through the Spirit. For the Spirit searches everything, even the depths of God."

NOTE DISTRACTIONS & REMINDERS:

THOUGHTS, PICTURES, WORDS, OR SONGS THAT COME TO MIND:

ACTIONS TO TAKE:

SCRIPTURE ON WHICH TO MEDITATE:

Revelation 3:11 ESV
I am coming soon. Hold fast what you have, so that no one may seize your crown.

NOTE DISTRACTIONS & REMINDERS:

THOUGHTS, PICTURES, WORDS, OR SONGS THAT COME TO MIND:

ACTIONS TO TAKE:

WHAT IS GOD SAYING TODAY?

SCRIPTURE ON WHICH TO MEDITATE:

Romans 8:1 ESV
There is therefore now no condemnation for those who are in Christ Jesus.

NOTE DISTRACTIONS & REMINDERS:

THOUGHTS, PICTURES, WORDS, OR SONGS THAT COME TO MIND:

ACTIONS TO TAKE:

WHAT IS GOD SAYING TODAY?

SCRIPTURE ON WHICH TO MEDITATE:

John 7:16 ESV

"So Jesus answered them, "My teaching is not mine, but his who sent me."

NOTE DISTRACTIONS & REMINDERS:

THOUGHTS, PICTURES, WORDS, OR SONGS THAT COME TO MIND:

ACTIONS TO TAKE:

SCRIPTURE ON WHICH TO MEDITATE:

Amos 3:7 ESV

"For the Lord God does nothing without revealing his secret to his servants the prophets."

NOTE DISTRACTIONS & REMINDERS:

THOUGHTS, PICTURES, WORDS, OR SONGS THAT COME TO MIND:

ACTIONS TO TAKE:

WHAT IS GOD SAYING TODAY?

SCRIPTURE ON WHICH TO MEDITATE:

Luke 18:27 ESV
But he said, "What is impossible with man is possible with God."

NOTE DISTRACTIONS & REMINDERS:

THOUGHTS, PICTURES, WORDS, OR SONGS THAT COME TO MIND:

ACTIONS TO TAKE:

WHAT IS GOD SAYING TODAY?

SCRIPTURE ON WHICH TO MEDITATE:

Your Luke 18:27 ESV
"But he said, "What is impossible with man is possible with God."

NOTE DISTRACTIONS & REMINDERS:

THOUGHTS, PICTURES, WORDS, OR SONGS THAT COME TO MIND:

ACTIONS TO TAKE:

WHAT IS GOD SAYING TODAY?

SCRIPTURE ON WHICH TO MEDITATE:

Matthew 6:33 ESV
"But seek first the kingdom of God and his righteousness, and all these things will be added to you."

NOTE DISTRACTIONS & REMINDERS:

THOUGHTS, PICTURES, WORDS, OR SONGS THAT COME TO MIND:

ACTIONS TO TAKE:

WHAT IS GOD SAYING TODAY?

SCRIPTURE ON WHICH TO MEDITATE:

Job 23:10 ESV
"But he knows the way that I take; when he has tried me, I shall come out as gold."

NOTE DISTRACTIONS & REMINDERS:

THOUGHTS, PICTURES, WORDS, OR SONGS THAT COME TO MIND:

ACTIONS TO TAKE:

WHAT IS GOD SAYING TODAY?

SCRIPTURE ON WHICH TO MEDITATE:

Ephesians 1:18 ESV

"Having the eyes of your hearts enlightened, that you may know what is the hope to which he has called you, what are the riches of his glorious inheritance in the saints,"

NOTE DISTRACTIONS & REMINDERS:

THOUGHTS, PICTURES, WORDS, OR SONGS THAT COME TO MIND:

ACTIONS TO TAKE:

WHAT IS GOD SAYING TODAY?

SCRIPTURE ON WHICH TO MEDITATE:

Psalm 107:28 ESV
"Then they cried to the Lord in their trouble, and he delivered them from their distress."

NOTE DISTRACTIONS & REMINDERS:

THOUGHTS, PICTURES, WORDS, OR SONGS THAT COME TO MIND:

ACTIONS TO TAKE:

SCRIPTURE ON WHICH TO MEDITATE:

1 Peter 5:8 ESV
"Be sober-minded; be watchful. Your adversary the devil prowls around like a roaring lion, seeking someone to devour."

NOTE DISTRACTIONS & REMINDERS:

THOUGHTS, PICTURES, WORDS, OR SONGS THAT COME TO MIND:

ACTIONS TO TAKE: